HANDS-ON ROBOTICS™

THE HISTORY OF ROBOTS AND ROBOTICS

MARGAUX BAUM AND JERI FREEDMAN

rosen publishing's rosen central®

New York

Published in 2018 by The Rosen Publishing Group, Inc.
29 East 21st Street, New York, NY 10010

First Edition

Library of Congress Cataloging-in-Publication Data

Names: Baum, Margaux, author. | Freedman, Jeri, author.
Title: The history of robots and robotics / Margaux Baum and Jeri Freedman.
Description: New York : Rosen Publishing, 2018 | Series: Hands-on robotics | Includes bibliographical references and index. | Audience: Grades 5–8.
Identifiers: LCCN 2017026424| ISBN 9781499438932 (library bound) | ISBN 9781499438925 (pbk.) | ISBN 9781499439380 (6 pack)
Subjects: LCSH: Robotics—History—Juvenile literature. | Robots—History—Juvenile literature.
Classification: LCC TJ211.2 .B385 2018 | DDC 629.8/9209—dc23
LC record available at https://lccn.loc.gov/2017026424

Manufactured in the United States of America

CONTENTS

INTRODUCTION

Humans have always imagined artificial people or mechanical humanoids—commonly known as robots—that would perform tasks similar to those performed by people, and even envisioned ones that had humanlike thoughts and motivations.

After hundreds of years of dreaming of and dreaming up robots, humanity has succeeded this past century in transforming science fiction into science fact. Robots were deployed onto factory floors in the twentieth century. These days, robots stand poised to make an impact on battlefields and crime scenes, in hospitals and hotels, in banks and restaurants, on the roads and in households.

Robotics is a field that will see many breakthroughs in the near future that will far surpass the advances of the last few decades. Mechanics, electronics, and software make up the three main areas of robotics that will likely transform our society and culture dramatically.

Artificial "humans" of one kind or another have existed in many different cultures since the beginning of recorded history. For much of this time, they were envisioned or conceived as replacements for people, machines that would do work in humans' place.

Robots have certainly captivated novelists, filmmakers, and other creative people throughout the centuries. Many books, films, and other texts have featured robot characters. Some are helpful and friendly, like the droids from the *Star Wars* franchise of films, the lovable title character of *Wall-E*, or the robot housekeeper Rosie from the 1960s animated sitcom *The Jetsons*. Others have been fearsome, and have expressed human fears of technology, including the assassin robot in *The Terminator*

The popular imagination of what robots look like has varied widely over time. Here is a recent interpretation—the title character from the 2008 computer-animated science fiction comedy *Wall-E*.

films, and many other science fiction, horror, and thriller movies. The fear of robots either enslaving humanity in some way, or stripping us somehow of our very humanity has also been a favorite aspect of many speculative robot stories.

Many robot narratives have been more ambiguous. Robots may end up serving food in fast food and other eateries, cleaning hotel beds, processing humans' applications at government offices, and be involved in many other tasks and processes in our society that may displace workers and also challenge the way we have done things for a long time.

The real-life robots we may encounter in our lifetimes may be both frightening and friendly, from firearm-equipped law enforcement robots and hovering military drones, to more pet-like contraptions, like mechanical family pets that perform programmed tasks and even provide companionship. To understand where things are going for humans and their robotic creations, however, it will be helpful to track where our conceptions of robots arise from, how actual robotic technologies have evolved over time, and what place robots have in our present-day society, and what promise they hold for tomorrow.

CHAPTER ONE

BEFORE ROBOTS

The Czech writer and playwright Karl Čapek coined the term "robot" in 1920, in a play called *R.U.R.* (which stood for "Rossum's Universal Robots"). It depicted artificial people created in a factory. Derived from the Czech word for work (*robota*), specifically forced labor performed by feudal serfs (servant farmers in medieval times), the concept of the robot was most tied to work.

The industrial age at the time had changed production from a small-scale affair in the eighteenth century into a massive endeavor, with many automated mechanical systems now doing the work of many men. In these systems, many thinkers observed, men also became more like machines.

In the later twentieth century, actual robots came online and replaced human beings in many industrial processes. While automation definitely wiped out many former working-class jobs before, in recent years this process has accelerated. According to Ball State University's Center for Business and Economic Research, 85 percent of the 5.6 million factory jobs that disappeared from 2000 to 2010 were lost due "to technological change—largely automation."

Robots can be stationary, like those that assemble products on an assembly line, or mobile like the Mars Rover, scouting the terrain of remote locations. Some of the most fascinating robots are those that mimic life—whether they are robotic insects designed in a Massachusetts Institute of Technology (MIT) lab, or humanoid robots, like ones created by Japanese automaker Honda's research labs.

The basic mechanical principles that allowed the development of automated machines and robotlike mechanisms were laid down well before modern times. The ancient Greeks were especially skilled at creating mechanical devices. Ancient Greek texts provide a record of a number of automated machines, including construction cranes, catapults, and water clocks with moving figures produced by Ctesibius (ca. third century BCE).

AUTOMATION IN ANTIQUITY

In the third century BCE, a work called *Mechanics* was written in Greece. It is attributed to the philosopher Aristotle (384–322 BCE). *Mechanics* describes a number of devices that are key to automating machines: levers, rollers, and gears, simple and compound pulleys, and other mechanical components. These basic devices are still used today in machines.

Archimedes (287–212 BCE), another Greek philosopher interested in engineering, invented the worm gear. A worm gear is a cylinder of metal with grooves like those in a screw that interlocks with a conventional round, toothed gear and turns it. Among other advantages, this type of gear allows small, normally weak motors to produce more force to manipulate appendages on a machine.

Figures and devices that move on their own mechanically are called automata. This is from the Greek word *automaton*, which means "self-acting" or "self-operating." Automata were used in the theater as far back as ancient Greece. In his work on automata, Hero of Alexandria (10–70 CE) recorded a number of automata used in theatrical and religious presentations, including moving figures and devices that produced sounds and flames. In the first century BCE, the Roman engineer Vitruvius recorded several automata as well.

This drum adorned with automata made to resemble a child and a clown is a relic from late nineteenth-century Germany.

All of these early automated devices relied on pulleys, pumps, pistons, gears, and levers to produce motion. Although today's robotic machines are controlled by electronic rather than mechanical means, the moving parts still consist of these types of mechanical components. A controller is a device that manages the overall movement of the parts of a mechanical or electronic device. Early controllers were mechanical. For example, a windup mechanism that turns gears that move a figure's arms and legs is a mechanical controller. An electronic controller does the same thing for modern robots, but it has a continuous power source, such as electricity from a battery or a power line.

THE GOLEM: ARTIFICIAL MAN

The concept of a human-sized artificial man was first described in Jewish folklore. This creation was called the golem, and there are several versions of its story. One of the most often recounted stories involves the head rabbi of sixteenth-century Prague, now the capital of the Czech Republic.

The rabbi constructed an artificial man of clay in order to protect the Jews who were being persecuted by the local authorities. The golem was brought to life by writing the name of God, or the word *emet* (Hebrew for truth or reality), on its body. (In some versions of the story, the word is written on a piece of paper placed under the golem's tongue.) Not unlike a classic robot, the golem could not think on its own but carried out tasks literally, according to the instructions it was given. When the intimidated Prague authorities agreed to stop their persecution of the city's Jewish population, the golem was deactivated by erasing or removing the word from the golem's body. The similarities to a programmable robot or artificial intelligence remain clear.

MEDIEVAL AUTOMATION

After the decline and fall of classical Greece and Rome, many Greco-Roman texts made their way to North Africa and the Middle East. Arab scholars collected and preserved them. They were inspired by these works, and took many of their ideas and concepts further. Around 800 CE, the caliph of Baghdad commissioned the *Book of Ingenious Devices*, which collected all the Greek knowledge and writing about mechanical devices. It describes the construction of about one hundred mechanical devices, including an automated flute, which is considered to be the first programmable device because it could be set to play different tunes.

In 1206, Al-Jazari (1136–1206) wrote the Persian-language work, *The Book of Knowledge of Ingenious Mechanical Devices*, which describes designs for air- and water-driven machines and automata. One example from the book is a device intended to dispense wine and water at parties. This device included an automated servant girl, an automated horse and rider, and an automated serving man. In China and Japan inventors at the royal courts also produced a variety of automata, including birds, animals, and moving figures.

The Renaissance saw the dawning of a new era of scientific and logical inquiry into natural phenomena, and the sciences of mechanics and physics advanced from the fourteenth through eighteenth centuries. Knowledge of mechanics and physics flourished partly due to their preservation in Arab texts, enabling the first steps toward the invention of simple, programmable devices.

Programmable devices are machines that can run without human intervention or control after being given a set of instructions. Early machines were programmed mechanically. For example, imagine a music box that is wound up, causing a gear to turn, which makes a set of metal teeth contact different pins to produce various notes to play a song. This music box could be programmed to play a different song by changing the settings of its pins.

DA VINCI'S "ROBOT"

Italian artist and inventor Leonardo da Vinci (1452–1519) learned about the human body from anatomical studies. Around 1495, he combined this knowledge with information on mechanics from

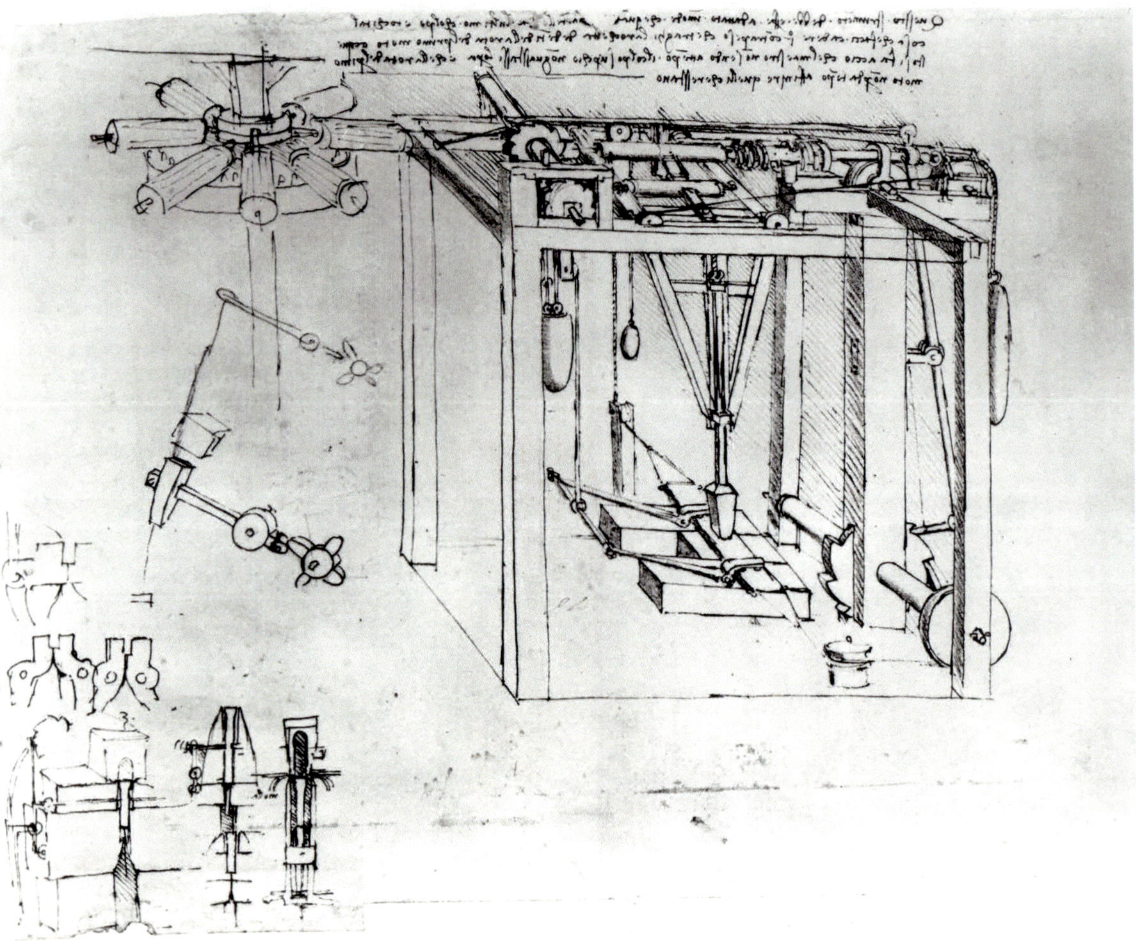

Renaissance inventor and thinker Leonardo da Vinci sketched this prototype of an automated hammering machine in a notebook, one of many ideas he had that could qualify as early predecessors to robotics.

ancient Greek texts to design, and some say build, the first version of a robot. It was a robot knight dressed in armor.

Leonardo's robot was designed to sit up and move its head and limbs to the accompaniment of automated drums. Made of wood, metal, and leather, its parts were operated by a series of cables, gears, and pulleys connected to a mechanical controller in its chest. The same general principles are applied today to move the head and limbs of humanoid robots, although the controller today would be electronic rather than mechanical.

Leonardo da Vinci was not the only person to build a robot during the Renaissance. In 1540, Gianello Torriano (1515–1585) built a mechanical woman that played the mandolin, and in 1772, P. Jacquet-Droz (1721–1790) built a mechanical child that could write on paper with a pen.

EARLY COMPUTING MACHINES

Robotics could not fully come into their own, however, until the development of the first computers and their ability to store and process complex instructions. The first steps toward building a working computer were taken during the Renaissance as well.

In 1642, Blaise Pascal (1623–1662), for whom the computer language Pascal is named, designed the first machine to perform arithmetical functions, thus producing the first computing machine. It used a series of gears inscribed with numerals and a ratchet device. This device could incrementally move a gear when it reached the digit 9, allowing the machine to perform addition and subtraction mechanically.

Gottfried Wilhelm Leibniz (1646–1716) invented a way to allow the automatic calculator to perform multiplication. He did this by using repeated addition to simulate multiplication. This principle

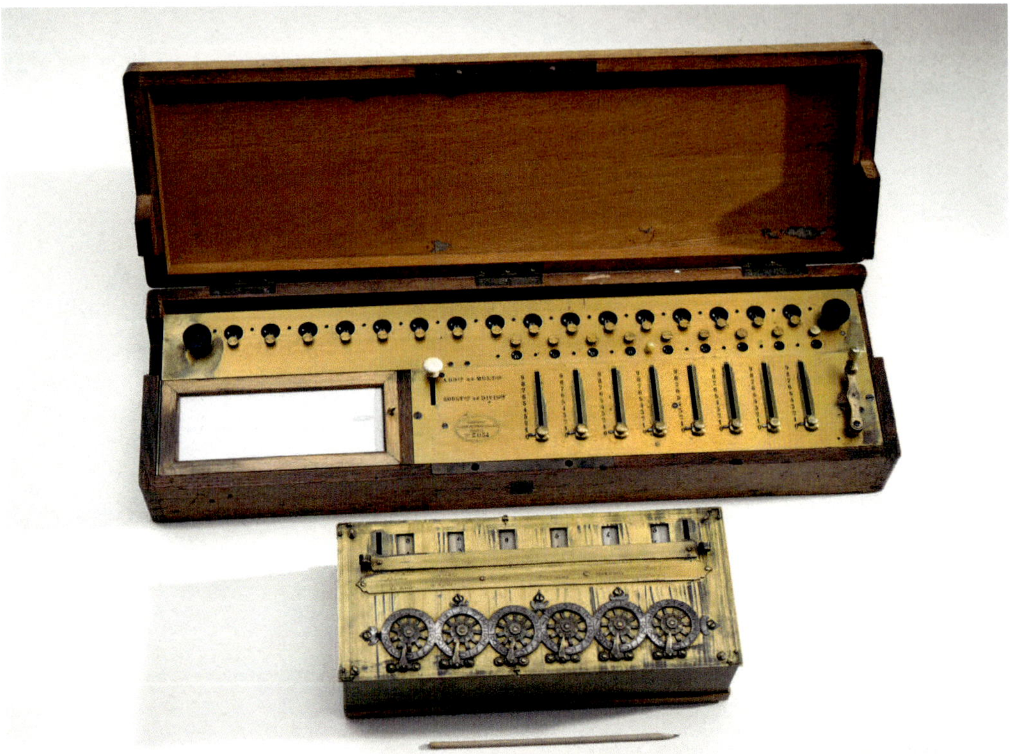

Here is a replica of the original calculating machine that French physicist and mathematician Blaise Pascal built in 1642. It was designed to perform addition and subtraction.

was later used in electronic computers. Leibniz also suggested that using a two-digit system rather than a ten-digit system would make performing automated mathematical calculations easier. This approach was resisted by scientists of the time, but over a century later George Boole (1815–1864) developed a two-digit system, called binary. Today, it forms the basis of processing by all modern computers.

CHAPTER TWO

THE ERA OF AUTOMATION

During the nineteenth century, scientific progress in the physical sciences led to the creation of the electronic technologies that made twentieth-century (and modern) robotics possible. The Industrial Revolution that began in England and later swept the world, especially the young nation known as the United States, marked the end of individual craftsmen handmaking goods for sale. Instead, large and automated systems were set up to mass produce goods. Around this time, inventors first tried their hand at creating robots that could potentially perform the same work as human beings.

AUTOMATED PRODUCTION

Today, robotics is closely associated with the programmed machines that can quickly mass produce consumer products, including items like cars. The roots of these industrial robots and the computers that control them can be traced to the early nineteenth century. During this time, steam engine technology reached a stage of development that made automated machines practical to use in factories.

In 1805, Joseph-Marie Jacquard (1752–1834) invented the first programmable automated production machine. He used a series of cards with holes punched through them to control the patterns made by an automatic loom used in textile production. Each hole or lack of hole in a card was read as "on" or "off" by the machine. This same type of binary punch card system would later be used to program early computers. Today's computers are programmed in basically the same manner, but the "on/off" signal is a "1" or "0" sent digitally, rather than a hole punched in a card, which is also transmitted many times faster.

EARLY INNOVATIONS

English engineer Charles Babbage (1791–1871) wrote a paper in 1821 titled, "Observations on the Application of Machinery to the Computation of Mathematical Tables." Babbage explained how it would be possible to construct a machine that could calculate astronomical tables automatically. He then set about building a prototype of his idea. Although his concept was sound, the difficulty of obtaining the necessary precision parts at that time kept him from completing the project. Nevertheless, Babbage's "difference engine" is considered the first physical conceptualization of a computer.

In 1877, William Thomson (1824–1907), known as Lord Kelvin, built the first practical computer. An avid yachtsman, he wished to calculate information about the tides. He figured out the formulas necessary to accomplish this, but the calculations were lengthy and time consuming. He thought it would be possible to build a machine to perform them instead of doing so by hand. In 1876, using wires, pulleys, and dials, Thomson built a machine that, when a crank was turned, calculated the tides along the harbor. It could predict a year's worth of tides in four hours.

Charles Babbage created one of the first fully-automated calculating machines, known as an Analytical Engine, just before he died in 1871. Pictured is a trial model of what Babbage envisioned.

AUTOMATED LABOR

In 1868, engineers Zadoc P. Dederick and Isaac Grass created a steam-powered man who pulled a cart. This was followed by the development of steam-powered mechanical men of various sorts by a number of other inventors. One such inventor was George Moore of Canada. In 1893, he produced a steam-powered man

ROBOTS: BORN IN LITERATURE

The first mention of robots in literature might be in the *Iliad* by Homer. When the god Hephaestus entertains the goddess Thetis in his home, Homer writes: "There were golden handmaids also who worked for him, and were like real young women, with sense and reason, voice also and strength, and all the learning of the immortals; these busied themselves as the king bade them."

From the nineteenth century through the twentieth century, actual robots have appeared frequently in literature. However, the modern concept of a robot is more closely associated with Isaac Asimov than any other writer. From the 1940s on, he wrote stories that featured robots. In 1940, he even coined the term "robotics" in one such story. His most notable contribution to the concept of robots, however, was his formulation of the "Three Laws of Robotics" in his 1943 short story, "Runaround". These laws have formed the basis for many ideas about how robots should behave, and some version of one or more of them has popped up in many science fiction stories, films, and television shows since. According to Asimov's laws:

- A robot may not harm a human being, or, through inaction, allow a human being to come to harm.
- A robot must obey the orders given to it by human beings, except where such orders would conflict with the First Law.
- A robot must protect its own existence, as long as such protection does not conflict with the First or Second Law.

who could walk at speeds of up to 5 miles (8 kilometers) per hour.

However, the invention of electric power as a practical source of energy to run machines spelled the end for much interest in steam-powered robots. In modern times, the concept of the mechanical laborer would be combined with advances in automated machinery to produce the industrial robot, capable of performing complex tasks previously performed by human workers.

Isaac Grass and Zadoc Dederick built this steam-powered robot in Newark, New Jersey, in 1858. It was called the Newark Steam Man and inspired similar steam-related inventions of the era.

DAWN OF THE ROBOTS

Advances in electronics, cybernetics, and computer science led to the creation of functional robots. Improved electronics made it possible for control devices to use signals to communicate with robots. Cybernetics is the technology of communicating with, and receiving feedback from, machines such as robots. Cybernetics allowed for the creation of more sophisticated robots that were better able to interact with their surroundings. Computer science encompasses the writing of computer software and algorithms to provide instructions to electronic machines such as robots. All three of these areas are key to the development of modern robots.

CYBERNETICS AND FEEDBACK

Cybernetics enabled the development of advanced robots. This was the final stage in developing a modern "controller" for robotics. Today, a controller is understood as a device that not only controls the speed, motion, and force of an automated machine, but also adjusts these in response to feedback from the robot. Feedback is registered by sensors that measure elements of the robot's performance such as direction, force, and speed, among others. This self-adjustment makes it possible for the robot to work without human intervention, and respond to the physical environment, and its own limitations in it.

During the 1940s, mathematician Norbert Wiener (1894–1964) worked with engineer Julian Bigelow (1913–2003) to create control systems for antiaircraft guns. These guns had to be able to swivel in order to track the movement of passing planes. Wiener observed that, in order to control the movement of the guns' components, it was necessary for the system to have some means of feedback that would allow it to tell what motion was occurring. This would allow the antiaircraft gun to adjust itself accordingly for different movements. In 1948, Wiener wrote a book called *Cybernetics: or the Control and Communication in the Animal and the Machine*, in which he presented the idea that one could simulate biological and social responses in inanimate objects by using sensors to provide feedback to machines.

US soldiers man an antiaircraft gun at a desert air base during the Allied military campaign in North Africa during World War II. Some of the feedback systems used in certain antiaircraft systems were ahead of their time.

Warren McCulloch (1893–1969), director of the Neuropsychiatric Institute at the University of Illinois, became interested in Wiener's ideas. He wanted to combine elements of neuroscience, mathematics, and engineering to create machine systems that could mimic human behavior. In 1952, McCulloch moved his research team to MIT to work on cybernetics. The basic areas of cybernetics were developed at MIT: machine perception, learning, memory, regulation, and adaptation. This research laid the foundation for artificial intelligence and modern robotics.

CHAPTER THREE

ELECTRONICS AND AI

While cybernetics provided an important leap forward toward automation, advances just on the horizon that would help human beings create machines that truly emulated human abilities and actions. The early to middle twentieth century was a time of great progress in electronics and early computing. This era was marked by the leap from simple mechanical systems to electronics.

Electronics were circuits or devices that made use of transistors and chips, with electricity as the power source. Switches would switch on or off in response to electric signals to create messages and program parts of machines to move or execute other tasks. Now, more sophisticated calculations and tasks could be accomplished. Electronic components provided the foundation for many things, including radio technology, and helped usher in modern robotics.

Many of these advances were made during World War II and were part of the government-funded war effort. Some of the earliest modern computers were designed by the Allies in order to crack German codes. In 1940 at Iowa State University, John Atanasoff (1903–1996) and Clifford Berry (1918–1963) developed the first true electronic computer, called the Atanasoff-Berry Computer, or ABC.

During the war, a group of British code breakers was tasked with deciphering messages written by the Germans. The German code was known as the Enigma code, created by using a device called the Enigma machine. The British developed Heath Robinson, a code-breaking computer, and later in 1944 the first of the Colossus series of computers. These early computers could perform mathematical operations very fast, but they could not be programmed.

In 1945, the Electronic Numerical Integrator and Computer, or ENIAC, was completed. It was the first programmable computer. ENIAC was designed by J. Presper Eckert (1919–1995)

Codebreakers work at Bletchley Park, the intelligence center of the British war effort, in 1943. They were charged with cracking the secret Enigma codes of the German Nazis.

and John Mauchly (1907–1980) at the University of Pennsylvania Moore School of Electrical Engineering and funded by the U.S. Department of Defense (DoD). Unlike a computer that could merely be set up to run through a series of calculations faster than a human being could, ENIAC used subroutines. By using subroutines, a computer can be programmed to perform different activities depending on the result of a calculation. After completing the subroutine, the computer returns to the main program. This breakthrough significantly increased the processing ability of computers by allowing them to perform different functions according to the result of a given processing step.

ENIAC (Electronic Numerical Integrator and Computer), shown here with operators tending to its various systems, was the first electronic digital computer, first introduced in February 1945.

Mathematician John von Neumann (1903–1957) developed the concept of storing data and instructions in a computer's circuitry. He coined the term "memory" to describe this kind of data storage. Von Neumann's work became the basis for the Electronic Discrete Variable Computer (EDVAC) created at the University of Pennsylvania in 1951. It still forms the basis for how computers operate today.

In the mid-1950s, computer technology took a giant leap forward with the development of the transistor. A transistor is a tiny piece of semiconducting material, such as silicon, with terminals attached to it that conduct electricity. Groups of transistors used together form an integrated circuit, more commonly called a computer chip. The development of technology to print microscopic circuits on silicon made it possible to string together a large number of circuits in a very small space, vastly increasing the processing capabilities of computers. Today, computer chips are made by printing vast numbers of such circuits on a wafer of silicon that is cut into tiny pieces—hence the term, "computer chip."

ROBOTIC AUTOMATION MOVES FORWARD

One of the most influential people in the development of industrial robotics was George Devol (1912–2011), who created the first electronically controlled robotic arm in 1954. He also developed a magnetic recording system that could read instructions from a drum coated with magnetic material. This is the same basic principle used in computer hard drives today. In 1955, Devol and Joseph F. Engelberger (1925–2015) formed a company to manufacture commercial industrial robots. The company was called Unimation, or universal automation. Devol used the term "universal automation" to describe a type of robot that could be programmed to perform a variety of tasks.

In the mid-twentieth century, researchers began to develop techniques that would allow machines to learn and to mimic human actions and responses. Their goal was a machine that could not only perform a programmed task over and over, but also learn and adapt so that it could perform more complex functions, similar to those performed by human workers. This mimicking of human thought was called artificial intelligence, or AI.

Machine learning is at the heart of artificial intelligence. Machine learning is based on the premise that every aspect of learning can be formulated precisely enough that a machine can simulate it. Artificial intelligence allows machines to acquire information, make decisions based on the accumulated information, and then produce output based on its decision.

Alan Turing was a pioneer of theoretical computer science, inventor of the Turing machine, and was instrumental in using codebreaking to shorten World War II.

EARLY AI

In 1937, British mathematician Alan Turing (1912–1954) proposed that a computer could perform any problem-solving or decision-making task a human being could. He developed the concept of a computer that could acquire knowledge the way a human being does. He also proposed that, if a human being engaging in a conversation with

A MACHINE THAT REALLY THINKS?

In 1993 the Humanoid Robotics Group at MIT, led by Rodney Brooks, started work on Cog (short for "cognition"), a robot designed to learn the way that a human beings does. This meant that Cog learned through interaction with its environment, including other human beings. Doing so required the ability to perceive and draw conclusions, skills that are difficult to instill in a robot.

In order for Cog to interact with people, it was necessary to get people to interact with the robot. To this end, the lab gave Cog a head with features that could convey expressions the way human faces do. This ensured that people would interact with it naturally. The researchers also tried to find a way to imbue Cog with an understanding of social skills that would allow it to interface naturally with people.

Writing in an academic paper, "Theory of Mind for a

The Australian roboticist Rodney Brooks is shown here in 1996 with Cog, the robot that "learned" through experience.

Humanoid Robot," Brian Scassellati, an MIT Intelligence Lab scientist who worked on the Cog project, "Normal social interactions depend upon the recognition of other points of view, the understanding of other mental states, and the recognition of complex non-verbal signals of attention and emotional state." Therefore, the project had to find a way to give Cog the ability to recognize and interpret these elements.

a computer cannot tell whether he or she is conversing with a person or a machine, then the machine could be considered intelligent. This has become known as the Turing Test. Turing's work spurred an interest in developing machines that could "think" like human beings.

In 1943, Warren McCulloch (1893–1969) and Walter Pitts (1923–1969) developed a mathematical model of "neural net" computing. This would prove to be key to the development of artificial intelligence. A neural net mimics the network of interlinked neurons in the brain.

In an artificial neural network, processing elements, referred to as nodes, are linked together, working together to perform tasks. The more that given nodes are used together, the stronger their relationship becomes. The advantage of neural networks is that they allow the use of approximation, which lets a machine operate on incomplete data. For instance, a neural network computer can estimate a high likelihood that a certain action is correct or that a certain image represents a flaw in a component without having to be programmed to understand something that exactly matches what it encounters. In this way, a neural network can simulate the way that human beings make judgments based on partial information.

PROGRAMMING AI

New computer languages were invented to allow computers to process information efficiently enough to make AI possible. In 1959, John McCarthy (1927–2011) and Marvin Minsky (1927–2016) founded the AI lab at MIT, one of the facilities that has led artificial intelligence research. At the lab, John McCarthy developed LISP, one of the first programming languages that could be used for AI. Using LISP, a computer searched a massive list of possible solutions to a problem repeatedly until it found the best one. It is said that McCarthy first coined the actual term, "artificial intelligence," while Minsky is remembered by many as the "father of artificial intelligence."

In the 1960s, AI researchers started work on developing expert systems. This work, which has continued to the present day, is focused on accumulating large databases (repositories of data) on various subjects, such as medicine or geology, and developing rules that allow computers to make judgments about the information. These rules are intended to simulate the way in which human beings think.

CHAPTER FOUR

MOBILE ROBOTS AND BEYOND

Before the 1960s, most examples of robotics included stationary machines that performed certain actions in industrial settings. But that would soon change, as technology improved to make moving, humanoid robots possible.

The first freestanding and mobile robots were relatively simple. Begun in 1966 and completed in 1972 at the Stanford Artificial Intelligence Laboratory, Shakey was a wheeled machine on a platform, equipped with a television camera, and some remotely linked sensors and components. Still, Shakey navigated a small, enclosed space independently, which was a huge milestone.

By 1984, the Stanford lab had split from Stanford University, and was now an independent entity, the Stanford Research Institute. It developed a robot called Flakey, which had stereo vision (meaning it could see through two eyes and then combine those visual inputs), a computer program that allowed it to interpret speech, and a sophisticated system of sensors that allowed it to receive information from its environment. Flakey could follow people around and use its speech recognition system to respond to spoken commands.

The computerized robot named Shakey was capable of very simple but autonomous reasoning. Charles Rosen, shown here with Shakey in 1970, served as project manager working for SRI International.

NASA, THE MILITARY, AND ACADEMIA

One of the big supporters of mobile robot development was the National Aeronautics and Space Administration (NASA), which hoped to develop robots to explore the surfaces of other worlds. In 1966, the first robotic space explorer, Surveyor, landed on the moon. NASA continues to fund the development of mobile robots. In 2001, MD Robotics of Canada's Space Station Remote Manipulator System was launched to complete assembly of the International Space Station. In 2003, two NASA Mars Rover robots landed on the surface of Mars. Designed with treads that would allow them to traverse uneven surfaces, the Mars rovers were equipped to gather geological information.

Another big impetus for the development of mobile robots came from the United States military. It wanted to create robots that could go into enemy territory and move about intelligently on their own. These robots would handle supply delivery, scouting, and potentially even combat missions.

Beginning in 1984 the U.S. Department of Defense's Defense Advanced Research Projects Agency (DARPA) began to fund research into robotic automated land vehicles, or ALVs. Much like human drivers, these completely automated vehicles process visual information and use a variety of mapping systems to navigate roads and terrain. The earliest effort was NavLab, a Chevy van rigged with computer equipment.

One of the key scientists involved in the development of NavLab was William Red Whittaker, director of Carnegie Mellon University's Field Robotics Center. Whittaker and his associates also built robots to work on the cleanup in the wake of the Three Mile Island nuclear power plant disaster in 1979 and the Chernobyl nuclear power plant disaster in the Ukraine in 1986. In 1986, Whittaker founded his own company, RedZone Robotics, Inc.

This mobile inspection robot, known as Pioneer, is shown exploring the still-radioactive site of the 1986 Chernobyl nuclear disaster in Ukraine sometime in 1999.

Whittaker developed robots that could work in hazardous environments. His teams at the Carnegie Mellon University field lab created robots that have searched for meteorites in Antarctica and explored Mars's surface. In the 1990s, one of his teams came up with a six-legged walking robot to explore the Mount Spurr volcano in Alaska.

In the twenty-first century, companies began working on mobile robots for personal use as well. Carnegie Mellon University's robots and people team have been working on developing a service robot that can assist patients and the elderly. GeckoSystems Mobile Service Robot line is also designed to help the elderly. Gecko's robots, called CareBots, can navigate independently and communicate verbally. In 2009, iRobot (maker of the vacuuming robot Roomba), established a health care unit to work on developing an eldercare robot.

In 2009, scientists at the Intel Lab at Carnegie Mellon University held a public demonstration of HERB, the House Exploring Robotic Butler. HERB is still a work in progress; the researchers are designing the robot so it will be able to analyze and navigate its environment, respond to commands, and manipulate objects, all without human intervention.

TWO-LEGGED LOCOMOTION

Ever since people first thought about building artificial versions of living organisms, they desired to make one in the form of a human being. One of the major problems with making a humanoid robot, however, is that it must walk on two legs. People must constantly adjust their bodies to maintain balance while moving. For a humanoid robot to function successfully, it would need to do the same.

Serbian engineer Miomir Vukobratovic, developed a concept in 1970 to cope with this problem. He called it the Zero Moment Point, and it refers to the point at which the various forces that affect the robot's stability are in balance. Japanese scientists and engineers used this concept to pioneer humanoid robots.

Later, in 1973, Ichiro Kato's bioengineering group at Waseda University in Tokyo, Japan, created the first humanoid robot, Wabot-1. Wabot-1 had artificial eyes and ears and even an artificial mouth. It could communicate in Japanese and grasp objects with its hands, which were equipped with tactile sensors. In 1984, the same group produced Wabot-2, a robot that could play music. Wabot-2 could see the notes on a sheet of music, process this information, then play the notes, using its hands to play the keys of an electric organ and its feet to press the pedals of the instrument.

On February 14, 2002, Honda's humanoid robot ASIMO rang the bell to open trading on the New York Stock Exchange (NYSE) in honor of the twentieth anniversary of the trading of Honda's stock on the exchange—and more than twenty years of Honda's working on creating a humanoid robot. According to Honda, "At the NYSE ceremony, the 4 foot ASIMO robot ascended a set of stairs on the bell podium, shook hands with NYSE Chairman and CEO Richard Grasso, rang the opening bell and waved and clapped along with hundreds of traders on the floor of the Exchange." Honda's ultimate goal is to create a robot that can move and behave just like a person in order to act as a service robot. Honda began its research efforts in 1986.

Walking is not the only human motion robots can emulate, as demonstrated by this robot known as the Murata Boy. it was named after its creators, the Nagaokaky, Japan-based Murata Manufacturing.

Honda worked on the E (for experimental) series of robots from 1987 to 1992. The company wanted to develop the technology that would enable robots to walk. In 1993, they began working on prototype bipedal robots, and in 1997, they debuted the P3, an independent 5-foot (1.5 m) walking robot. The P3 represented a major advance in bipedal robots, but it still had to stop to negotiate challenges like making sharp turns. Honda's ASIMO robot, though, can walk continuously the way a human being does, using real-time feedback to guide its adjustments. Not to be outdone, Sony Corporation debuted the SDR-4X humanoid robot at the computer

BABY ROBOTS

In a sure sign that robots were moving into the mainstream, in 2001 both Mattel and Hasbro introduced robotic baby dolls. These dolls could do things like blink, cry, and simulate sleep. The two toymakers took different approaches to their toys. Hasbro's was more sophisticated, being able to call, cry, coo, and even mature. However, it looked more like a robot than a living baby. Mattel's toy was more limited in what it could do, but it resembled a traditional baby doll. Mattel's decision to go for a less robotic and more human appearance was the result of studies with children. These showed that children wanted a doll that looked human more than they wanted additional functionality. Such discoveries subtly influence the direction of robotics. Machinelike robots may be adequate for factory use; however, personal robots, or those that interact directly with people (especially consumers) are more widely accepted if they are more human-looking.

convention Robodex in 2003. The SDR-4X can sing and dance and even gave a performance at the convention.

FROM ROBONAUTS TO THE NEXT GENERATION

In 1997, NASA began development work on Robonaut at the Dexterous Robot Lab at the Johnson Space Center in

NASA's Curiosity Mars rover is shown here taking a self-portrait at the Namib Dune location on the planet Mars, on January 19, 2016. Many similar robotc probes will likely enter space this century.

Houston, Texas. Robonaut, a legless humanoid robot, is intended to assist astronauts inside and outside space stations and vehicles. In 2010, NASA and General Motors jointly introduced Robonaut 2 (R2), a stronger and more versatile version of Robonaut. R2 can even use some tools used by human workers. "Working side by side with humans, or going where the risks are too great for people, machines like Robonaut will expand our capability for construction and discovery," Mike Coats, the director of the Johnson Space Center, said in a statement on the NASA website.

We have not yet reached the point where robots look and perform like people, but all the inventions and technologies thus far have contributed to progress in this direction. There is little doubt that as we continue through the twenty-first century, researchers will move ever closer to the creation of a fully functional humanoid robot.

GLOSSARY

algorithm A mathematical rule used in computer programming.
anatomy The physical structure of the body
android A robot that looks like a human being.
appendage A limb, real or artificial.
automaton A machine that looks and acts like a human being.
binary A mathematical system that uses two states (on or off; 0 or 1) to encode data and instructions used by a computer.
caliph A title given to medieval Muslim rulers of Baghdad.
compound pulley A combined fixed and movable pulley.
controller A device that coordinates the actions of mechanical components in a device.
database A collection of data stored on a computer.
entities Physical beings.
humanoid Having the shape of a human being.
inanimate Not living.
mechanics A branch of science that deals with the movement of objects.
physics A branch of science that deals with the physical properties of objects and the forces that act on them.
piston A mechanical component that consists of a disk or cylinder that fits tightly in a cylindrical casing and pumps air or fluids.
programmable Capable of using a sequence of instructions to carry out an activity.
ratchet A mechanical component that moves other components up and down in steps.
semiconductor A material that conducts electricity but does so less well than metal.
sensor A device that is sensitive to sound, light, pressure, or another physical characteristic. Sensors send signals to a monitoring or controlling device.
simulate To imitate or model.

FOR MORE INFORMATION

Computer History Museum
1401 North Shoreline Boulevard
Mountain View, CA 94043
(650) 810-1010
Website: http://www.computerhistory.org
Twitter: @ComputerHistory
Facebook: @computerhistory
In addition to on-site exhibits covering computer history and technologies, the Computer History Museum maintains an illustrated history of the computer online.

FIRST Robotics Competitions
200 Bedford Street
Manchester, NH 03101
(800) 871-8326
Website: https://www.firstinspires.org
Twitter: @FIRSTweets
FIRST robotics competitions are among the most well known of their kind nationwide and internationally, and their websites provides information about past challenges, upcoming contests, and scholarship opportunities.

IEEE Robotics and Automation Society
445 Hoes Lane
Piscataway, NJ 08854
(732) 562-3906
Website: http://www.ieee-ras.org
Twitter: @ieeeras
A national society, the Robotics and Automation Society is part of the Institute of Electrical and Electronic Engineers (IEEE),

and offers professional and student chapters that focus on advancing innovation, education, and research dealing with robotics and automation.

MIT Humanoid Robotics Group
545 Technology Square
Cambridge, MA 02139
(617) 253-5851
Website: http://www.ai.mit.edu/projects/humanoid-robotics-group
MIT conducts some of the most advanced research in robotics in the United States, and has some of the industry's most cutting-edge labs and collections of scholars, including the Humanoid Robotics Group.

Robotics Society of Southern California
800 North State College Boulevard
Fullerton, CA 92831
Website: http://www.rssc.org
Facebook: @roboticssocietyofsoutherncalifornia
YouTube: https://www.youtube.com/user/RSSCRobotics
The RSSC organizes its own competition each year and is one of the biggest societies by membership in the USA.

Seattle Robotics Society
P.O. Box 1714
Duvall, WA 98019-1714
Website: http://www.seattlerobotics.org
A nonprofit enthusiasts' group whose members include amateurs and professionals, high school students and college professors, the Seattle Robotics Society offers newcomers to robotics online chat sessions and information on getting started with projects.

Western Canadian Robotics Society
c/o The Hangar Flight Museum
4629 McCall Way NE
Calgary, AB T2E 8A5
Canada
Website: http://www.robotgames.com
Facebook: @WCRS.YYC
The Western Canadian Robotics Society is dedicated to the advancement of "personal robotics" and organizing robotics competitions in Western Canada.

WEBSITES

Due to the changing nature of internet links, Rosen Publishing has developed an online list of websites related to the subject of this book. This site is updated regularly. Please use this link to access the list:

http://www.rosenlinks.com/HOR/History

FOR FURTHER READING

Brasch, Nicolas. *Robots and artificial intelligence*. Mankato, MN: Smart Apple Media, 2011.

Chaffee, Joel, and Margaux Baum. *Engineering and Building Robots for Competition* (Hands-on Robotics). New York, NY: Rosen Publishing, 2018.

Greek, Joe. *Artificial Intelligence* (Digital and Information Literacy). New York, NY: Rosen Publishing, 2018.

Hustad, Douglas. *Discover Robotics*. Minneapolis, MN: Lerner Publications, 2017.

La Bella, Laura. *The Future of Robotics* (Hands-on Robotics). New York, NY: Rosen Publishing, 2018.

Mara, Wil. *Robotics Engineers* (Cool STEAM Careers/21st Century Skills Library). Ann Arbor, Michigan: Cherry Lake Publishing, 2015.

Parker, Steve. *Robots in Science and Medicine*. Mankato, MN: Smart Apple Media, 2011.

Payment, Simone, and Margaux Baum. *Building a Career in Robotics* (Hands-on Robotics). New York, NY: Rosen Publishing, 2018.

Peppas, Lynn. *Robotics*. New York, NY: Crabtree Publishing, 2015.

Ryan, Peter K. *Powering Up a Career in Robotics* (Preparing for Tomorrow's Careers). New York, NY: Rosen Publishing, 2015.

Spilsbury, Louise, and Richard Spilsbury. *Robotics*. New York, NY: Gareth Stevens Publishing, 2017.

BIBLIOGRAPHY

American Society of Cybernetics. "Noted Contributors to Cybernetics and Systems Theory." Retrieved March 4, 2010. http://www.asc-cybernetics.org/foundations/cyberneticians.htm.

Cocco, Federica. "Most US Manufacturing Jobs Lost to Technology, Not Trade." *Financial Times*, December 2, 2016. https://www.ft.com/content/dec677c0-b7e6-11e6-ba85-95d1533d9a62.

Honda Motor Company. "Honda's Advanced Humanoid Robot 'ASIMO' Makes U.S. Debut." February 14, 2002. Retrieved March 7, 2010. http://asimo.honda.com/NewsArticle.aspx?XML=News/newsarticle_0008.xml.

Kurweil, Raymond. "The Age of Intelligent Machines, Chapter Five: Mechanical Roots." KurzweilAI.net. Retrieved March 2, 2010. http://www.kurzweilai.net/articles/art0314.html?printable=1.

Maia, Matara J. *The Robotics Primer*. Cambridge, MA: MIT Press, 2008.

Massachusetts Institute of Technology. "Cog." Retrieved March 8, 2010. http://www.ai.mit.edu/projects/humanoid-robotics-group/cog.

Nadajarian, Gunalan. "Islamic Automation: A Reading of Al-Jazari's *Book of Knowledge of Ingenious Mechanical Devices* (1206)." Foundation for Science, Technology and Civilisation. Retrieved March 3, 2010. http://www.muslimheritage.com/uploads/Automation_Robotics_in_Muslim%20Heritage.pdf.

NASA. "R2." Retrieved March 7, 2010. http://robonaut.jsc.nasa.gov.

National Science Foundation. "HERB, the Robot Butler." February 1, 2010. http://www.nsf.gov/news/special_reports/science_nation/robotbutler.jsp. Nocks, Lisa. *The Robot: The Life Story of a Technology*. Baltimore, MD: John Hopkins University Press, 2008.

Peppe, Rodney. *Automata and Mechanical Toys*. Wiltshire, England: Crowood Press, 2002.

Rosheim, Mark E. "Leonardo's Lost Robot." Institute and Museum of the History of Science. Retrieved February 28, 2010. http://brunelleschi.imss.fi.it/genscheda.asp?appl=LIR&indice=63&xsl=sezione&lingua=ENG&chiave=100955.

Russell, Stewart. *Artificial Intelligence: A Modern Approach*. Upper Saddle River, NJ: Prentice Hall, 2009.

Shankland, Stephen. "Intrepid Robot Set for Chernobyl Mission." CNET News, May 28, 1999. http://news.cnet.com/Intrepid-robot-set-for-Chernobyl-mission/2100-1001_3-226504.html.

Waseda University Humanoid Robot Institute. "Wabot." Retrieved March 7, 2010. http://www.humanoid.waseda.ac.jp/booklet/kato_2.html.

Wood, Gary. *Edison's Eve*. New York, NY: Random House, 2003.

INDEX

R

S

T

ABOUT THE AUTHOR

Margaux Baum is an editor and author from New York, with many published credits on technology geared toward young adult readers.

Jeri Freedman has a BA degree from Harvard University. For fifteen years she worked for companies involved in cutting-edge technologies. She is the author of more than thirty young-adult nonfiction books, including *Careers in Computer Science and Programming* (Careers in Computer Technology), *Digital Career Building Through Skinning and Modding*, and *Intellectual Property* (Cyber Citizenship and Cyber Safety).

PHOTO CREDITS

Cover Chad Ehlers/Photographer's Choice/Getty Images; p. 5 AF archive/Alamy Stock Photo; p. 9 DEA/A. Dagli Orti/De Agostini /Getty Images; pp. 10, 28, 37 (background) Sylverarts Vectors /Shutterstock.com; pp. 12, 14, 17 Science & Society Picture Library/Getty Images; p. 19 Science History Images/Alamy Stock Photo; p. 21 Margaret Bourke-White/The LIFE Picture Collection /Getty Images; p. 24 Bletchley Park Trust/SSPL/Getty Images; p. 25 Historical/Corbis Historical/Getty Images; p. 27 Heritage Images/Hulton Archive/Getty Images; p. 28 Ted Thai/The LIFE Images Collection/Getty Images; p. 32 Ralph Crane/The LIFE Picture Collection/Getty Images; p. 34 © AP Images; p. 36 Koichi Kamoshida/Getty Images; p. 38 NASA/JPL-Caltech/MSSS.

Design: Michael Moy; Photo Research: Karen Huang